This Book Belongs To:

_____

Books Created by Glow:
Dr. Chloe Cupcake: Counts to 10
Dr. Chloe Cupcake: Shapes
Dr. Chloe Cupcake: Colors
Dr. Chloe Cupcake: Alphabets
Dr. Chloe Cupcake: Counting to 20
Happy Birthday Dr. Chloe Cupcake
Dr. Chloe Cupcake: Sight Words
Dr. Chloe Cupcake: Following Directions

Cory's School Bus: Meet his buses
Cory's School Bus: Counts to 10
Cory's School Bus: Teamwork
Cory's School Bus: Colors
Cory's School Bus: Counting to 20
Cory's School Bus: Alphabets
Cory's School Bus: Sight Words
Cory's School Bus: Following Directions

ISBN: 9798626469837

Dedication

This book is dedicated to Tabitha Brown and the Brown Family.

Hi! I am Doctor Chloe Cupcake and when I grow up, I will be a Doctor.

I would like to tell you a little bit about what I eat.

Our family eats a plant-based diet. This means we only eat plants, no meat or meat products.

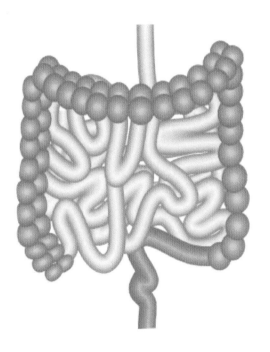

We eat plants because it is good for us. This diet helps our digestive system.

I know that you are wondering where we get our protein. That's an easy one! We get our protein from plants.

Plants build our bodies to be big and strong. Think about some of the animals that only eat plants.

Look at the elephants, they only eat plants and they are huge. Elephants are big and strong.

We don't just eat salads. Mommy and Daddy Cupcake make all kinds of meals.

We eat at some restaurants too.

My favorite meal is a veggie burger and fries.

Adding a little cheese, made from plants. Mmmmmm

My favorite fruits are strawberries and blueberries. My favorite veggie is sweet potato because I love sweet potato pie.

My favorite snack, is a fruit parfait.

You can do so much with a plant-based diet.

No matter what your diet is, it is very important that you eat plenty of fruits and vegetables.

What is your favorite meal?

Do you like fruits and vegetables?

I love my diet and I hope
you get a chance to try it.

The End

Made in the USA
Monee, IL
08 May 2021

67120588R00017